First published in Great Britain by HarperCollins Publishers Ltd in 1996. ISBN 0 00 198149 8 (hardback) 10 9 8 7 6 5 4 3 2 1
ISBN 0 00 664540 2 (paperback) 10 9 8 7 6 5 4 3 2 1 Text and illustrations copyright © Ian Beck 1996
of HarperCollins Publishers Ltd, 77-85 Fulham Palace Road, Hammersmith, London W6 8JB. Printed and bound in Italy.

POPPY AND PIP'S WALK

Ian Beck

Collins

An Imprint of HarperCollins*Publishers*

The sun was shining.
Poppy called, "Pip, let's go for
a walk, there's time before tea."

Poppy and Pip set off for their
walk, over the hill and far away.

Past the pond, Poppy said,
"This way Pip."

Pip said, "Woof."

Someone said, "Quack."

Through the gardens, Poppy said, "Hurry up Pip."

Pip said, "Woof."
Duck said, "Quack."

Someone said, "Miaow."

Into the woods, Poppy said,
"Oooh, scared Pip?"

Pip said, "Woooof!"
Duck said, "Quaaaack!"
Kitten said, "Miaowwww!"

And someone said, "Tweeeeet!"

In the bright field, Poppy stood still,
Pip stood still, they all stood still.

Poppy said, "A little bird, a little kitten, a little duck. We must take them all home again."

"Woof, woof," said Pip.

First they took the little
bird back to the nest.

"Tweet, thank you,"
said the mummy bird.

Then they took the little kitten
back to the gardens.

"Miaow, thank you,"
said the mummy cat.

Then they took the little
duck back to the pond.

"Quack, thank you,"
said the mummy duck.

Poppy and Pip went back over the hill and home.

It was tea time.

"Mmmm," said Poppy.
"Woof, woof, woof," said Pip.

Make friends with the
C☻llins **Toddler** stories

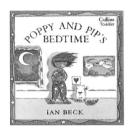
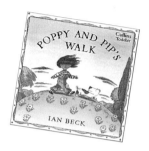